This animal legend was told by the Aborigines of Australia. Whales really do have lice. The legend also adds that from that day to this starfish have had to hide among rocks and pools so that the whales cannot find them.

BLACKIE CHILDREN'S BOOKS

Published by the Penguin Group
Penguin Books Ltd, 27 Wrights Lane, London W8 5TZ, England
Penguin Books Australia Ltd, Ringwood, Victoria, Australia
Penguin Books Canada Ltd, 10 Alcorn Avenue, Toronto, Ontario, Canada M4V 3B2
Penguin Books (NZ) Ltd, 182-190 Wairau Road, Auckland 10, New Zealand

Penguin Books Ltd, Registered Offices: Harmondsworth, Middlesex, England

First published 1993
10 9 8 7 6 5 4 3 2 1
First Edition
Copyright © 1993 Joanna Troughton
The moral right of the author has been asserted

A CIP catalogue record for this book is available from the British Library

ISBN 0–216–94027-3

First American edition published in 1993 by
PETER BEDRICK BOOKS
2112 Broadway
New York, NY 10023

Library of Congress Cataloging-in Publication Data is available for this title

ISBN 0–87226–509-9

Filmset in Monotype Baskerville

Printing arranged by Imago Productions (F.E.) Pte. Ltd., Singapore

FOLK TALES OF THE WORLD
WHALE'S CANOE
A FOLK TALE FROM AUSTRALIA

RETOLD AND ILLUSTRATED BY

JOANNA TROUGHTON

Blackie Children's ... ... Bedrick/Blackie
London ... New York

Long ago, before the animals lived
where they do now, the birds flew over a
beautiful new land. It was full of forests,
wide plains, mountains and winding rivers.

The birds told the animals
on the opposite shore about
the beautiful new land
across the sea.

They all wanted to go there.

Each animal had a small canoe, but none was strong enough for the big ocean waves.
The only canoe that was strong enough was . . .

. . . Whale's canoe!

The animals were all frightened of Whale.
He was very bad-tempered and mean.
'Can we borrow your canoe?'
they asked nervously.

'No,' said Whale. 'Certainly not.'

Then Starfish said to Whale: 'I see your head is full of lice. Let me pick them off for you.'

Whale agreed. His head was very itchy.

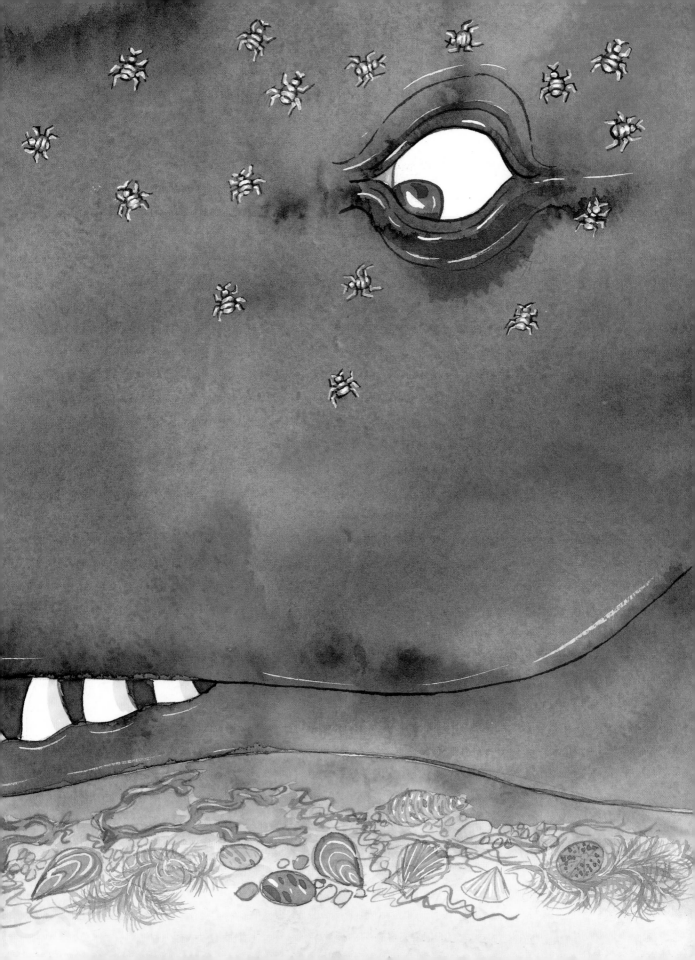

Starfish picked off the lice with her delicate
fingers. Whale's eyes closed. Soon he was
fast asleep.

'Quick!' said Starfish to the animals.
'Get Whale's canoe!'

The animals paddled Whale's canoe
through the big ocean waves.

But Whale woke up.
  'My canoe is gone!'
he roared.
And he chased the animals.

Whale chased them almost to the opposite shore.

Crane quickly broke Whale's canoe. He danced on it until it was just a pile of broken bark.

Now Whale's canoe was broken, he could never come ashore. He must live for ever in the sea. The animals were safe in their beautiful new land, full of forests, wide plains, mountains and winding rivers. They called it Australia.